OMEGA FOR OBSESSIVE ALPHA

Wolf Shifter MPREG Fated Mates Romance

Michael Levi

ISBN: 9798799598747
Imprint: Independently published

1st edition

Cover design by: Michael Levi

CONTENTS

CHAPTER 1

Feran

I felt something sniffing me, like he was trying to smell me. I cracked open my eyes as I found someone standing right in front of me. It was a man, huge, older than me, and hot as balls. The moment my eyes set on him, it was like fireworks exploded in my head.

I wanted to rip his clothes off his body and see what he was like naked. I wanted to slide my tongue over his muscles, to feel him for the man he was, to grind my body against his, and to make sweet love with him. I was already drooling even though I didn't even notice that yet.

The guy who was in front of me was so close I could smell the minty odor coming out of his mouth. His eyes were emerald green, his hair messy and blond, some stubble on his chin.

His face was chiseled and followed hard lines, making me want to put my hand on it and feel it until he was smiling.

And I just noticed I was supposed to be falling to the floor.

I felt something holding me in place so that that didn't happen. It was his arm, wrapped around my torso. It was firm, showing off his confidence. I was still in the same room from before, which was behind the bar where I was drinking away my sorrows.

I just remembered something terrible that happened not too long ago, which made me come running to this place. I supposed I should be thankful he was holding me like this so that I didn't fall and hurt myself, but the way he was smelling me was also frightening and annoying. I should be shoving him away from me as fast as possible and as hard as I could, but that was easier said than done.

I wasn't going to say that I was skinny. In fact, I was lean and I did work out, but I didn't follow any diet and I didn't inject my body with anything. This guy, on the other hand, looked more like a gym rat than anything.

And he was even more frightening because his body was covered in tattoos. There was even one of them, which caught my attention the most, sneaking from under his shirt and going across his neck.

It was the tattoo of a lone wolf, making me remember that he was probably from *that* MC gang. I shivered at the thought of having caught the attention of one of them. It was the worst thing that could be happening.

Not to mention that I didn't have anything to do with him...

He parted his lips, blowing a bigger cloud of his mouth's odor over my face. I closed my eyes and scrunched up my nose, but not because I was turned off by the smell, but because his scent was overwhelming.

As an Omega, I was always subjected to this kind of situation, especially when the other guy was an Alpha. And it wasn't just the smell coming out of his mouth that was making me hard and aroused right now. It was also his musky scent, which came from all around his body.

"I just saved you from hurting yourself. I think you should be thanking me." And as soon as he finished saying that, he smiled, showing me his perfect teeth. I always thought that bikers like him didn't brush their teeth, but it looked like he was an exception.

I knew he was a biker because of the patch he had on the front of his leather jacket. It showed that he, indeed, was from one of the biker gangs in the region. They were called the Wolf Bikers, and everyone around here in the city feared them. They were a menace, robbing people and their houses, causing the police all sorts of troubles.

I knew that coming to this bar was a mistake, but I didn't think I was going to run into a member of the Wolf Bikers.

I shot my hands to his chest, shoving them against it. I thought he was going to leave me alone and add some distance between us, but he held his ground, tightening how hard his arm was pressing against my torso.

"Hey! Leave me alone!" I yelled, hoping that someone in the bar was going to hear me, but as time passed, I realized I was alone. I shouldn't even have come into this room to cry alone.

But when I was in the main room of the bar, some Alphas were bothering me. They couldn't keep their arousal in check when I stepped into the place, and thus they were hitting on me all the time. I grew annoyed and ended up stumbling into this room.

One curious thing about that was that this guy was not with them. Even though I was a little drunk, I was certain of that because those bikers were from a different gang. They were called the Bear Bikers, and they were even bigger of a problem than the Wolf Bikers.

"I don't think so, sunshine." His voice was low, throaty, almost like he was always grumpy. And yet, it was still sexy and very much like the kind of voice I liked in a man. "I know your family has a lot of money."

I locked my eyes with this, shivers running down my spine. The way he said that, it could only mean one thing.

I tried to shove him away from me again, only to find his strong and determined chest standing in my way once more. He didn't move, not even an inch. "I'm not going anywhere with you!"

He dipped his head, making me feel that his lips were going to connect to mine. And even though they were perfect lips that made me want to kiss him over and over, I wasn't going to fall for that.

I wasn't going to let my feelings for him get in the way of what I was supposed to do. I needed money for the operation, and I was going to get it, one way or the other.

I did remember something interesting and a little frightening, which I was trying not to think about. I sure as hell didn't want to think that it was true. My father once said that I was going to marry someone I was meant to be with. He said that I was fated to be his, that God wanted things to be that way.

I punched that thought out of my mind right away. My father said that when he was better and also when he was on his death-bed. It meant a lot to him that I married the right Alpha, which was one reason why I was willing to be with anyone who wanted something more long-term with me.

The only problem with that was that nobody wanted that. Everybody was always just looking for a quick fuck.

"I didn't say I was going to kidnap you, but now that you brought it up, I think I just might," he growled, bringing his arm up so that I was standing, and then pushing me forward until we were crossing the door out of the bar.

Moments later, my feet were crunching over the grass and my eyes were greeting the glow of the moon. I looked around, scream-ing out of my lungs as I hoped that someone was going to save me.

But no one was. We were in one of the most forgotten neigh-borhoods in the city, where not even the cops came here. I would be lucky if anyone even opened their window to find out what was going on.

His hand shot to my mouth, shutting it. He dipped his head until his lips were next to my left ear. "Stop yelling or I'm going to hurt you, and you really don't want to find out how much I can hurt."

Shivers ran down my spine again when I realized I was hearing something loud coming in our direction. Snapping my head to it, the first thought that came into my mind was that it was a cop, on a motorcycle, who witnessed what was happening.

I blinked twice, clearing up my vision, only to realize that it wasn't the police. It was just another biker, from the Bear Bikers gang.

He was on his motorcycle and was riding it like he was the king of the world. Pulling over, he pulled a pistol out of his leather jacket and pointed it at the kidnapper.

He pulled up the left corner of his lips before affirming, "Thanks for bringing him out, but this one is mine."

I crept my head around to glance at my kidnapper. Fur was beginning to grow on his face, his teeth becoming larger and pointy.

I already knew he was a wolf shifter, but I never thought he was going to transform right in front of me. He was already large and much bigger than me in his human form, and now the difference was becoming frightening. Much, much more. He made me feel tiny and unforgettable before him.

The Bear biker on the motorcycle cocked his gun, widening his smile. "You think you can survive a silver bullet to the heart? I'm not going to hold back on pulling the trigger, if I have to."

I thought the Wolf Biker was going to continue his transformation and fight against the other guy, but he did the opposite. Moving his arm away from me, he put his hand behind my back and shoved me forward, forcing me to stumble across the grassy field until I fell into the arms of the Bear Biker.

The latter wrapped one of his arms around me, revved up the motorcycle, and rode away after shoving me into the backseat while keeping his gun pointed to the wolf shifter.

Still drunk, the combination of everything happening with me was too overwhelming, and before long, I was closing my eyes and I couldn't reopen them.

I passed out and I had no idea what was going to happen.

CHAPTER 2

Yel

I stomped hard onto the grass, my fangs growing bigger. Fisting my hand, I couldn't help but feel like punching that bear biker until blood was gushing out of his mouth. I was going to bash his head against the pavement until his skull cracked, I swore.

I couldn't believe I was so amateur about it. I should have realized someone was going to come after him, too. I was going to make bank by kidnapping Feran.

Stomping on the grass again, all I could do was turn back and stride over to Delight, my bike. It was parked in front of the bar.

The members of the Wolf Bikers didn't know that I was here. They didn't frequent this part of town. I was the only one here, and the only one who should have known about Feran.

He was from one of the most important families in the city. I knew that kidnapping him would make me a lot of money. I didn't even feel bad about it, and I wouldn't either way. The money his family would have to hand over wouldn't even dent their fortune, after all.

I couldn't lose this opportunity.

The moon high above the buildings and the houses, I looked up at it as I realized how easy it would have been to turn into a wolf while that Bear Biker was pointing his gun in my direction. In a fair fight, did he think he would win?

Fuck that guy. He'd always been a nuisance. He was keeping tabs on me.

Ennith…

I was going to punch his gut so hard one day he would puke whatever was in his stomach, I swore, swinging my leg over Delight and remembering all the things that happened between us.

All the clashes we had, even when he was in school and trying to prove to the teachers he was better than me at pretty much anything. He joined up with the Bears because they were the right fit for him.

Turning on the engine of the motorcycle and propelling it forward, crossing one red traffic light after the other without even putting on my helmet, I was focused on just one thing – finding Ennith and Feran. I was pretty sure I knew where he was taking him to.

The Bear Bikers' hideout.

It wasn't too far and even though I wasn't going to have the support of the Wolf Bikers, I should be okay. I didn't need them, anyway. I was pretty confident in how well I could sneak in and out of that place. It was pretty big, with ample free space. I was going to have to keep my guard up all the time, but it wasn't a challenge impossible to tame.

I smirked, feeling overconfident. I had my gun with me now. I'd left it in the motorcycle because I didn't think I was going to have to use it during the kidnapping. I thought it was going to be simple.

Feran was pretty small, a little lean, weak, and very submissive. Me being the Alpha I was, he was always going to smell me and fall to his knees when his nose got a sniff of it. I mean, everything was going according to plan before Ennith popped up.

I couldn't help but feel aroused by Feran, though. He had short, dark hair, perfect lips, ocean-blue eyes, and lips that were just the right size.

When I enclosed my arm around his torso, the first thought that popped up in my mind was how much I wanted to rip the clothes off his body and bend him over. It only didn't happen because raping was something I would never do.

He was about 10 years younger than me, too. That was a piece of information I dug out on the internet. And that age gap was a plus for me, too.

If we had met under different circumstances, I'd be going for him for sure. The only problem with that was that now he thought of me just as an asshole who was trying to kidnap him.

Being the person I was, I couldn't care less about that.

I pulled up not too far from their hideout, pushing my motorcycle until it was hidden in a dark and forgotten alleyway between two massive buildings.

I pulled up my hood, shadowing my face, and went to one of the doors that two guards were by the side of.

Their hands went to their pistols as soon as they realized someone was padding over to them.

"Back off if you don't want to get hurt, jackass," one of them barked, pulling out his pistol when I swung my arm, striking him square on the side of his head. He fell limp on the floor, and I fished out his pistol before his partner could do anything. He stumbled backward, trying to pull the trigger of his pistol, but it was too late.

Yanking out my own pistol after storing the other I'd just snagged, I popped a bullet in his brain. The muffled sound caused by the silencer comforted me that nobody had heard anything. Smiling without showing my teeth, I searched their bodies until I found what I was looking for – the side door's key.

I opened it, snuck into the building, and then skulked down the hallways until I found the room I was looking for. After knocking out the guards protecting it, I crept open the door and found what I was looking for.

The Omega, strapped to a chair, still asleep. He was beaten up pretty badly. His face was covered in bruises and cuts, the region around his eyes bigger and swollen.

I felt a little bad for him, but not for longer than a couple of seconds. I went around him, sliced the rope on his wrists, and slapped his face so that he woke up. He flapped open his eyelids, snapping back to reality. "Wait, what?" He murmured, looking at me with dreamy eyes.

But then he panicked and started to struggle against the chair, almost toppling over. I yanked him to me before that happened and grabbed him with my arms, hugging him tightly.

"Woah there, little Omega. Not about to let you hurt yourself. After all, your family will pay less for you if that happens."

"I don't get it…" He murmured, closing his eyes all of a sudden and falling limp in my arms. I groaned, realizing that I was going to have to take him out of the building with me.

Sneaking through the guards had already been difficult without having to do that, and now it was going to be even harder.

I sighed, put him over my shoulders, and then went out of the room.

I skulked down the hallways, creaking open the door where I had come from. Inching my head outside, I turned my head left and right to see if anyone had come to see what happened here.

But I was so fast since entering the building that they hadn't had time to figure that out yet. The way ahead was clear, with no cars driving on the roads or pedestrians ambling on the sidewalks.

I smirked, closing the door behind me after remembering that I stored the bodies of those guys in a dumpster in the alleyway on the left. I placed Feran back on the ground, slapped his face until he reopened his eyes. He glanced me over, snapping his head from left to right as he tried to process what was happening.

The poor guy was still dazzled by the recent chain of events.

I put my arm around his shoulders, keeping him clutched to me as I took him to where I had left Delight.

And just when we were crossing the sidewalk to the next

block, I heard a shot coming from behind me.

CHAPTER 3

Feran

The shot echoed in the darkness, blood spilling out and smearing my face. I screamed, but I couldn't run away. I was frozen in place as I saw that a biker was running toward us. He had a pistol in his hand and was pointing it at the kidnapper again.

His body fell against mine, and I almost lost my balance and toppled over on the road with him. Locking his eyes with me, he muttered, "Take me to Delight. It's there – in the alley between those two buildings. Be fast about it because, otherwise, we won't have enough time."

I snapped my head in the direction he was pointing with his finger, still feeling his body a little too heavy against mine. The Bear Biker, running toward us, was still a significant distance away, and if I hurried up, we could get there before it was too late.

Problem was, I didn't think that was wise, nor did I think I should do that. After all, why should I help the guy that was trying to kidnap me?

The truth was that I shouldn't, but I also didn't know how to drive his motorcycle and I would be helpless in this neighborhood. It wasn't just that Bear Biker that was coming for us.

It was now a whole battalion of them, all sporting pistols and submachine guns. If I didn't hurry up and make a decision quickly, everything would be lost, and I and this guy would be locked up in the building again.

He slapped my face all of a sudden so hard it left a mark, my skin stinging. I had a choice of doing this on my own, most likely finding myself at the mercy of the Bear Bikers again, who probably had the same plans for me, or running away with this Wolf Biker, who was at least hurt.

I wasn't going to say that I had better chances of escaping if I chose the latter, but at least it made me feel hopeful.

It was like everything was happening in slow motion for me. Pushing my body forward, I dragged him across the sidewalk as we entered the alleyway. His motorcycle was parked there and nobody had seen it.

I peeked behind my shoulder and witnessed the Bear Bikers closing the distance. They were fast – faster than I thought they were, especially for guys so big who were already transforming.

Their fangs were popping out and their teeth were growing bigger, fur showing on their skin. Not too long from now, they were going to be not humans anymore, but bears, and I didn't want to stick around until then.

I took a deep breath, swinging my leg over the motorcycle and enclosing my arms around the torso of the biker. They had shot him in his belly, but the bullet had not gotten stuck inside of him.

Blood was still leaking through his clothes and I had no idea if he had enough energy to ride the bike back to where he lived. This was all a mess, which I could have prevented by not going to that bar in the first place.

The biker peeked over his shoulder, glancing at me. "Hang on tight. This is going to be a wild ride."

Hearing that, all I could do was what he wanted. Even though I felt disgusted that I needed him now, I pressed my head against his back and tightened up my arms around his torso. He twisted the handles of the motorcycle, propelling it forward and through the hoard of bikers running toward us.

More shots echoed in the darkness and all I could do was hope they weren't going to kill me or the biker trying to save himself. I could feel how strained and tense his body was, his skin growing warmer. I didn't like that, and it was making me worry he wasn't going to make it.

I closed my eyes tight until they were like slits, hearing the rumbling of the motorcycle's engine. The wind blowing against my face, I thought I wasn't going to make it too when I heard a bullet whizzing past my left ear. That was close. Too close.

My heart was pounding so hard I didn't even realize I was clutching on to my kidnapper, hoping that he was going to save me. I felt the motorcycle swerving, riding across the streets, and then going to a place that was underground.

The blowing wind was no more, the air around me growing colder all of a sudden. I cracked open my eyes, turning them left and right to figure out where I was. I couldn't even see the buildings and the houses that permeated the neighborhood where I had been. I couldn't even see the moon high in the sky anymore.

I was somewhere different, in a place underground like I thought before. I could see white fluorescent lights above our heads and pillars dotting the place. Turning my eyes left and right again, I could also see some cars and other motorcycles parked here.

We were in a parking lot under the building.

He peeked over his shoulder, glancing at me. Scrunching up his nose, I thought he was going to say something. For a moment, his eyes kept on looking at me and I had no idea how to react. It was the first time I was clutching on to a guy like this, feeling the hardness of his muscles under his leather jacket.

I moved away from him, getting off the bike as he tried to do the same. But as soon as his feet were on the ground, he lost his balance and fell over. Blood was still seeping out of his wound, and it looked like he wasn't going to make it.

I glanced around, hearing only the silence in the darkness of the parking lot.

I had the option of just running away and leaving him where he was, but then I saw that there were cameras in the parking lot.

Whether or not they were working, I couldn't know for sure right now. That meant if I ran away, the police would know I was involved in his death. Glancing down at him, I could see the pain in his face and that his eyes were losing their light.

He glanced at me, smiling as if he was mocking me – as if he knew what I was thinking.

"Take me to my room and I can erase every recording those cameras are making right now."

"Right, and then you'll lock me up and force my family to pay the ransom." I sighed, stepping away from him. "I can't do that. I don't want to put my family at risk."

He exhaled, pressing his hand against his wound. When he glanced back at me, he proposed, "Let's cut a deal. You will take me to my room, will help me get better, and then I'll let you go."

"How can I know you aren't lying? I don't trust you." I took another step away from him and was almost ready to get out of this place.

He pushed himself up until he was sitting on the floor. Even though he was smiling without showing his teeth, I could tell that the pain was eating him up from the inside. His face was paler than before.

"I'm giving you my word. You know that, as an Alpha, that means a lot to me."

He was right, but that still wasn't enough. What was, however, forcing me to help him was those damned cameras who were probably still recording this. I knew what the police were like in the city.

They would probably lock me up before even asking what happened and why I was involved in his death.

I felt a pang of pain when I realized how bad I would feel if I left him alone in this parking lot. I supposed I could call an ambulance, but then I'd have to give them my personal information, and I didn't want to take that risk.

No to mention that it would take them forever to get here. By the time the ambulance arrived, it would be too late for this Alpha whose name I didn't even know.

I shook my head, padding over to him as I grabbed his hand and helped him up. Chances were I was making the wrong decision, but from the looks of it, as long as he didn't die, I should still have enough time and a good opportunity to escape.

I couldn't believe I was helping my kidnapper, though.

CHAPTER 4

Yel

I cracked open my eyes, realizing that Feran was sleeping on the chair where he was sitting the night before. He didn't need to take the bullet out of my body. It sliced straight through the flesh, and it didn't hit any of my organs.

It just hurt like hell. And I supposed I should be thankful that this guy decided to help me even though the cameras in the parking lot had stopped working a long time ago. I wouldn't be living here if it had so much surveillance.

I sat on the bed, sniffing his scent. He smelled me too, which was one of the reasons I noticed he was hard that moment we met up at the bar. I was surprised he even decided to stay. I thought he was just going to leave me alone in the room.

I checked him out, from bottom to top, feeling a little bad that he spent so much effort healing me – going as far as dressing my wound – and I didn't do anything to help him, other than getting him out of the Bears' hideout, that was.

Everything was so quiet in the room and around the apartment building that someone would hear a pin falling to the floor. I was already feeling better, even though I could still feel some pangs of pain coming from where the bullet hit me.

Fucking Ennith. He always had to ruin everything and was always keeping tabs on me. Well, now he couldn't know where we were. I just moved into this project, and it would take the Bear Bikers and other gangs weeks before finding out about it.

If there was something the landlord prided himself in, it was that he kept everyone's secrets hidden and never ratted anyone out.

I thought that the Bear Bikers would have managed to chase me on their bikes, and even though I was pretty sure they tried, I didn't hear any of them getting anywhere near here.

The police weren't going to look too deep into what happened, and those filthy assholes that Ennith lived with weren't going to be much of a bother. That meant I should be safe.

I was an asshole. I'd admit that any day and I'd never lie about it, but I also... couldn't say that I didn't feel sorry for him. He shouldn't even be involved in this, and he wouldn't be so hurt now without my showing up in his life.

I got off the bed and nudged his shoulder, waking him up. He was a rich asshole who thought he was better than everyone, just like the rest of his family, but I wasn't heartless. His wounds needed to be dressed, and that's what I was going to do.

I wondered what would happen if he knew something that was once told to me a long time ago.

Feran cracked open his eyes, staring at me wide-eyed. He jumped off the chair where he was sitting, scooting away from me. I held up a hand so that he knew I wasn't going to hurt him.

The truth was, I had a softer heart than most people thought I had.

"Stay away from me!" He shouted, picking up a chair and brandishing it at me. "I made a mistake. I shouldn't have helped you. I should have run away when I had the chance."

I lowered my hand. "Does it look like I'm going to hurt you?" I queried, sighing. This was going to be a pain in the ass if he didn't give me another chance. "Plus, I've already changed my mind."

He lowered the chair, but didn't let go of it. Widening his eyes, he said, "What do you mean? I don't trust you."

I could smell his scent. It was perceivable, but not as strong as an Alpha's, as it wasn't supposed to be. I couldn't help but feel aroused by the way he was so scared of me, his pinkish lips, his rosy cheeks, and his jet-black hair. He was cute and my type.

"If I wanted to rope you to a chair, I'd already have done that." I locked my eyes with his, hoping that it was going to be enough to convince him.

He opened his hands, letting go of the chair. I proceeded to him, measuring the weight of my steps. Now that we were closer to where I wanted to be with him, I wanted to give ourselves a chance.

I could have at least a one-night stand with him, right? Just to wipe away the terrible thing I did today, and to thank him for dressing my wound...

"I suppose you're right," he murmured more to himself than to me, rounding the chair and sitting on it. I cracked open a gentle smile as I proceeded to him, grabbed everything I was going to need, and started to dress up his wounds.

Minutes later, when I was almost finished with that, I looked up at him. His eyes were avoiding mine, most likely wishing he didn't have anything to do with me.

"I'm sorry this had to happen to you."

"Now you are feeling sorry about it? My family is probably worried sick about me."

"I've got my phone with me. If you want to call them, you can."

Feran didn't say anything for the next few minutes, waiting until I was finished. I patted him on the shoulder when I finished dressing up the wound there. He looked to the left, muttering, "Thanks."

And it was at that moment, when his eyes went back to looking at me and I was holding his gaze, that our lips connected.

I was kissing the most handsome Omega I'd seen in my life, and it was washing away all the memories that came with me kidnapping him. I should never have done that.

My lips pressing and rubbing against his, I was taken by the strength of this moment and I couldn't think about anything else.

I drove my tongue into his mouth, put a hand on his waist, and pulled him up. I forced him to moonwalk until his back was bumping against the wall, a cloud of air escaping his mouth.

I thought he was going to protest and push me away from him, but Feran was actually immersing himself in the kiss. He was melting against me, and I was pressing my body harder against his. My hands roaming over his body, I couldn't help but start to pull up his shirt.

When I was mere moments from finishing that, he shoved his hand against my chest and made me scramble away from him. Feran was gasping for air when he asked, "What the hell was that?"

I smirked, settling both of my hands on the wall behind him. My face was so close to his we could kiss again and he wouldn't be able to do anything about it.

"Something I should've done a long time ago," I muttered, crashing my lips against his lips one more time and yanking his shirt off of him. His chest was finally bare before my eyes, my hands already going for it and groping it as I felt how smooth his skin was.

I didn't tell him this before, but he was my promised Omega. My father told me so before he died. I had always known that, and the whole kidnapping thing was just a ruse. Looking into his eyes, I could tell that Feran thought the same thing. He could almost read what I was thinking.

Our tongues battled inside our months, and I had control of the kiss soon after. I was overwhelming him, my hands groping him and sliding to where his nipples were. I pinched one of them, drawing out a profound moan from his throat.

I wasn't satisfied with that and thus decided to pinch his other nipple. He moaned again, squirming against my arms. His hands worked to yank off my belt, which he managed to do. I heard it fall to the floor moments later, my cock harder than it had ever been.

I couldn't believe that I was finally claiming my promised Omega, something I thought would never happen. My father said he was the one I had always been looking for, but for many years I didn't believe him, not until the moment when I met him in person for the first time.

His hands moved to my pair of boxer briefs, lowering it as he pushed it down. I stepped out of them, grabbing my dick and pointing it toward him.

He looked down, already getting to his knees. I could feel the hunger and thirst in his eyes, and also fear and desperation. I could tell it was the first time he was doing this, having sex with another man, and even though he was afraid, he was going on.

I was going to make this morning unforgettable for him.

CHAPTER 5

Feran

Light streaks snuck into the room, providing enough illumination so that I could make out what was happening. I was on my knees in front of a strong and overconfident Alpha, who had been in this kind of moment many times in his past. He was stroking his massive, impressive dong, and everything had been such a whirlwind I couldn't help but feel that this wasn't even the weirdest thing I did today.

The weirdest would definitely be saving this man's life just so that we could be doing this. I mean, I never planned for it.

He stroked my cheek and I lowered my head when he said, "You're my fated mate. You wouldn't be doing this if you weren't."

And he was right. While this was happening all of a sudden and it didn't make sense that it was, this man was the person I'd always been looking for all of my life. His musky scent told me so. The fact he dressed my wounds even though he didn't need to showed me the same.

One more thing made me believe that too, and it was the fact that I was getting wet for him. This wouldn't be happening if he wasn't my fated Alpha. I never felt so wet and hard for someone before, the thought of bending over and parting my legs for him permeating my mind...

"I know," I murmured, remembering how crazy this whole

thing was. One moment I was willing to kill him, the next he was dressing up my wounds, and now we were making love.

My hands were shaking. I didn't know what I was supposed to do. This being my first time, I felt like I was walking on eggshells. One wrong thing I did and I'd feel like I disappointed him, which was something I could never do to my promised Alpha.

The one.

My fated mate.

My heart pounding in my head, I wrapped my lips around his bulbous cockhead and worked it with my tongue, focusing on the lower region just under the tip. That's where he was most vulnerable and how I was going to win him over.

My other hand worked his balls as I noticed how low they hung. I played with them, wondering if he was thinking the same thing. Was he going to get me pregnant? I didn't know, but it was just something we – fated Alphas and Omegas – did, and it was like it was calling to me.

And the worst thing about this was that I didn't even know his name.

I didn't even realize he was moving until he was sitting down on the bed. Still with my mouth on his cock, I kept on swirling my tongue around his bulbous cockhead, tasting the pre-come that was coming out through the slit. It was salty and delicious.

My eyes were closed as I continued to work on his balls with my hand, my other hand roaming over his thigh as I felt his muscles and how hard they were.

I could do this for hours on end, if only I didn't have something else more important to do, but which I was keeping locked behind a closed door.

It wasn't long until his balls were hotter than they had ever been, his shaft throbbing in my mouth. My hand went over his thigh and then his abs, groping that part of him, which was so perfect. His muscles were hard and I just wanted to be feeling them with my hands for hours on end.

He moaned, throwing his head back as he felt, now stronger than ever before, that he was close to his orgasm. Bobbing up and down on his cock, his hands massaged my shoulders and kneaded my skin.

Pulling my hand back from his balls, I started to stroke my own dick fast, my hand shooting up and down in a blur. I was close to reaching my climax as well, but I was only going to do that when he was inside of me.

I pulled my head back, glancing down at his cock. His shaft was still mighty and hard, pre-come seeping out of the slit. I collected saliva in my mouth, letting it drool over his dick. He was all lubed up and ready to penetrate me.

My hole was already clenching at the thought of that happening.

I climbed up on him, inching my head to his. I could feel his hot breath on my face as I murmured, "Breed me. Knot with me. Make me yours."

He let out a hot cloud of air through his nostrils, grabbing my shoulders and spinning me around until I was lying down in the bed. He climbed up on top of me, pressing his lips against me one more time. His hands groped me and roamed over my body, kneading my skin.

"I'm going to do everything I can to make you happy," he promised, showing me that all the things he had been feeling for me this whole time were true. My suspicions were right.

I shuddered under his might, wishing he was already inside of me. I couldn't help but wish I already knew his name, but that was something for later.

He grabbed my thighs, shoved my legs over his shoulders, and then, in one fell swoop, impaled me. I felt his impressive cock breaching through every barrier my hole had. He barged through them like they were made of nothing.

In less than a fraction of a second, he was all the way inside of me, and I was holding his gaze for what felt like an eternity.

I tried to control my breathing, but it was almost impossible. My body was growing hotter as the seconds passed, and I could already tell this was going to be so painful I was going to be screaming through the whole thing.

The Alpha bent his body until his head was right above mine, teasing me for another kiss.

He parted his lips and asked, "How are you feeling?"

I closed my eyes, urging him to go on. "Better than ever, and I just want you to knot with me. Breed me."

Hearing that, he widened his smile and started to move in and out of me, his pace slow and controlled in the beginning. I matched him thrust for thrust, knowing that I was making the best choice of my life.

Yes, nothing of this made any sense, but it still felt right. I felt a strong and compulsive connection to this mighty Alpha because he was my fated mate.

His fur started to grow over his body, his teeth becoming pointed and bigger. The Alpha was reaching his orgasm and I knew that, when he was there, nothing would hold him back.

His massive cock grew even larger inside of me, knotting me like I'd begged of him. He peppered my neck with several kisses, and then picked up his pace when he felt he was closer. His balls slapping against my butt, I couldn't help but immerse myself in a world of dreams when my orgasm swept through my body like a tsunami.

I was gasping for air when the Alpha started to pump out his hot, thick load, coating my walls with it. It was perfect.

He was knotting me and breeding me, and I couldn't help but imagine what our child would look like. So many things to mull over, my family and other people getting worried sick about me, and that was the first thought popping up in my mind.

Truth was, it was the overwhelming joy and connection I felt to him that confirmed all of my suspicions. I was mating with my promised Alpha...

His shaft gave a couple of last spurts before beginning to lose shape and size. The Alpha pulled out, plopping on the bed and wrapping his arm around me. I pressed my lips to his, immersing myself in his strong and confident arms.

His body was as sweatier as mine was and we soaked the bedsheets wet. Moments later, I couldn't contain the rising urge surging in my mind, and I had to ask him an important question.

But just when I parted my lips to do so, he murmured, "I'm Yel."

And then it was when everything became clear to me.

YEL'S EPILOGUE

I pulled up the motorcycle, stopping in the parking lot by the hospital. Since that moment at the bar when everything happened, the last thing I thought would happen was me falling in love with him. But it was a different matter altogether when I found out he was my promised Omega.

He got off the bike, grabbing my hand when I pulled him by the scruff of his neck as I crashed my lips against his one more time. My father had always told me I was going to find my promised Omega, and I never believed him.

I never believed him until I looked at this man's eyes and I felt a strong, impulsive bond with him. It was then I knew he was the one.

And to think I had once planned on kidnapping him... I was out of my mind then.

He pulled his head back, and I grabbed his hand and squeezed it.

"Are you sure you don't want me to go there with you?" I asked, getting off the bike. It didn't matter what he said and what his answer was going to be. I was going to be nearby, even if I couldn't be right there on the same floor with him.

He shook his head, smiling gently and looking so cute he made me want to kiss him again.

"Don't worry about it. I'm going to be fine, really. I'm just going up there."

I sighed, settling my hands on his love handles as I neared my head to his one more time. I was smelling his scent, how it was calling to me, and how it made me want him more and more.

"You know I can't help but worry about you. I wasn't always looking for you, but now that I know we are meant to be together, I want to be with you all the time."

"I know," he murmured into my mouth, brushing his lips over mine for a fraction of a second. His hand moving down over my shoulders, I knew that this was the moment to part ways with him, even though it was only going to take a couple of hours. Those were going to be hours that were going to feel like an eternity to me, but that was okay. I could wait.

He turned around, padding over to the door of the elevator. I sighed, crossing my arms over my chest as I raked him with my eyes. I checked him out from bottom to top as I wished I was yanking off his clothes and making love with him one more time in our bed.

I turned off the motorcycle, went over to the wall by the elevator after it was already taking him to the floor where his father was, and leaned against the wall. I remembered when I was in the same situation he was. Losing one's father was never a good thing, especially when we needed their help the most.

I couldn't go up there because he was going to say his goodbyes to his father. I didn't like thinking about it, but it was true. His father couldn't go on the way he was, and he wasn't going to make it. He was going to say goodbye to him.

It was like time was passing by with the speed of a thunderbolt around me, and I reopened my eyes when I felt a scent I knew too well. My body grew tense all of a sudden, tensing up my shoulders.

I heard his motorcycle coming over, pulling up in the parking lot. My body was burning with the heat of a furnace, my fangs sprouting out. I was growing larger, approaching him.

I wasn't going to let Ennith ruin this. He wasn't going to.

I marched up to him, stopping right in front of him. His fangs were coming out too, fur growing on his body.

"Get out of my way," he growled, pushing me with his hand. I was doing everything in my power not to start a fight at the hospital. I didn't want to cause a scene.

"I'm not going anywhere," I barked, my jacket and shirt tearing up to pieces. My body was growing larger, begging me to get on all fours because it knew that the other side of me was coming out. When it was out, I couldn't control it, and I'd run rampant in the city. I couldn't let that happen. It wasn't going to.

His eyes assumed the shape and the color similar to those of a bear, his canines bigger as his body was now covered by his thick and brown fur. In a battle against a bear, I didn't know who would win, but I wasn't going to hold anything back.

"You don't want this fight to happen," he growled again, swinging his leg as he hit me and made me fall over on my side. I kicked him with the sole of my boot, right where his belly was. He reached for it, snarling at me.

"That was good, but it's not going to stop me." Ennith dashed toward me, bringing his elbow down with all of his strength. If I hadn't jumped out of the way, he'd have hit me and cracked open my skull.

I growled, howling when I lunged at him. I was already becoming more monster-like, my pants ripping to pieces as spits of my saliva flew in different directions. I climbed up on Ennith, roaring as just one thought permeated my mind like nothing before it did.

I knew what Ennith had come here for – or rather, *who*. He also wanted Feran. Wanted him for himself and to steal him from me, but only over my dead body.

I kicked him away from me with the sole of my boot, clocking him in the face as he lost his balance. Ennith fell over with a loud thud, his body already enormous and growing bigger still. His head's shape shifted, changed, and I could tell he was no longer human.

Now, more than anything, he was a bear, and he was going to

fight me like one. His nails were bigger and sharper, and he sliced the air with them as he cut my cheek. Pain surged in my body and spread to every part of me, making my eyes look red and blood-filled.

Ennith hurt me, and it only made me want to kill him more than I already did.

He jumped back up, bolting toward me as I readied myself and sharpened my fangs. I was going for his jugular, and nothing was going to stop me.

I stopped in my tracks when I heard the ding of the elevator, the doors sliding open. Out of it stepped Feran, widening his eyes when he noticed what was happening. It was a surprise to him that I was already in my semi-transformed form and fighting against someone he knew well. The bastard in front of me was the one who hurt him to the point of knocking him out cold.

Ennith leaped at me, pulling up his arm as he pointed his fangs toward my neck. I brought my arm up, ready to block it and slice his neck with my own fangs when we heard the cops' wailing sirens. They poured into the parking lot, pulling up.

Seeing that, Ennith reversed his transformation and got back on his motorcycle. There was an entrance that was still not blocked by the police cars, which he burst through on his motor-cycle. I stood where I was, gaping at him as he disappeared into the darkness of the city.

I reversed my transformation, my body going back to its human shape. I turned around, finding out that my Omega was running toward me.

He swung his arms around and buried his head on my chest, blurting out, "I had no idea he was going to come. I should've let you go up there with me."

I was naked like when I was born, feeling a little uncomfort-able with all the cops surrounding us. They were going to have many questions for me, and I had no idea if I was going to have all the answers they wanted. All I knew was that I was back with

Feran, who was still so special to me I kissed him again.

"Don't worry about it. I'm sure he won't be back. I'm going to make sure of it."

He softened up his eyes, tightening up our hug as he buried his head on my chest again. My heart slowing down, I could already feel much better than I was before. I could even pretend that the cops weren't around me, pointing their guns at us. They were afraid of the Alpha I was and what I could do.

People had always told me I was bigger and stronger than most other Alphas, which wasn't too far from the truth.

I kissed my Omega again and I knew that everything, from now on, was going to be much better.

FERAN'S EPILOGUE

I thought my father was going to have much more time than he did, but it wasn't meant to be. I was in front of his gravestone, hiding my tears as I felt the strong hands of my Alpha on me.

He had his hands on my shoulders, and he had been with me here for hours already. He didn't mention anything about that, but I still knew that it had already been hours since we came here.

"I'm sure he's proud of you," he murmured into my ear. My hand was roaming over my belly, which was now bigger than it had ever been. I was pregnant with Yel's baby and it was the most amazing moment in my life.

I took a deep breath in, turning around and burying my head on his chest just like it happened that one time he fought Ennith in the hospital's parking lot.

His arms were strong and as warm as they were then, bringing me the comfort and the support I was looking for.

I tilted my head up, gazing at his eyes. They were filled with his sense of understanding of what I was going through right now.

"It's over," he murmured, wrapping his arms around me and pulling me to him. "It's over and everything is going to be much better from now on."

I could feel his scent, his perfume, and how much he loved me.

"But I still feel like it's never going to be over. I feel like there's always something pulling me back."

"It's over like it is between me and Ennith. He'll never get out of that prison."

He was right about that. His sworn nemesis was locked up soon after that attack in the parking lot, and now there was no chance he could ever be released. I felt safe as long as he was in prison.

He moved his arm up, putting it over my shoulders as he took me away from my father's gravestone. We were soon out of the cemetery, and I turned so that I was facing him. He put his hands on my cheeks, kissing me one more time.

I felt that the kiss lasted for hours, when in reality it lasted just a handful of seconds.

He looked into my eyes, making the same question from before, "Everything's better now, don't you think?"

I nodded, not forgetting about my father's death, but remembering the good memories I had with him. He was always going to be in my mind, no matter what happened.

We strolled across the sidewalk to the parking space by the cemetery. He got on his bike, put on his helmet – which was something he didn't use to do before meeting me – and then revved up the motorcycle. He looked behind his shoulder, asking, "Want to go for a ride with me?"

I nodded again, burying my head in the crook of his neck. I was always ready for a ride with him on his bike, and it was something that would never change. Not to mention that today was far too bright and colorful for me to be depressed over my father's death. He was one of the most important people in my life and he was always going to be.

But now it was time for my life to take the next step and start anew. Settling my head in the crook of his neck, I felt his beating heart and how comforting it was.

He revved up the motorcycle again, riding off seconds after. I was riding through the city with him and it was the most amazing thing in the world. I could feel the wind blowing against my face and I didn't want this moment to ever end, no matter what happened.

I was with my fated Alpha and everything was going to be splendid from now on.

The End

Thank you for reading this story! If you enjoyed it, you can find more in this series:

Tasting the Omega 1: Rock-Hard

Tasting the Omega 2: Reckless Entry

Tasting the Omega 3: Rough in Public

Tasting the Omega 4: So Big It Hurts

Lastly, leave a review if you liked the book. It always helps me so much!

SNEAK PEEK: OVERWHELMING THE OMEGA

An Omegaverse MPREG Story (Lost Innocence - 1)

"Come on, Justin. It's yours if you want it," he said. His words were almost inaudible, though I didn't know if it was because of me, given the state of my mind, or because he was losing himself as well.

Slowly, but surely, I moved my shaking hand to his cock. It stood hovering above it for a few seconds before I dared to wrap my fingers around it. The moment they were locked around his big man tool, I sensed the thing throb slightly. Moments after, it was already growing in size.

His cock was warm - more so than the ambient air. It was so inviting to touch something so soft and tender. And I as I moved my hand a bit, I was rewarded by his toy growing a little bit. His balls moved when the side of my hand touched the skin of his sac. They went down a couple of inches, indicating the Hugo was getting in the mood.

Even though things had barely started, I moaned. My hand

moved up and down on his shaft. I was doing it slowly not to spook myself. I had no idea how big his toy could get. I also had no idea how loose his balls could be.

His shaft was not in a semi-solid state, though it was evident already that it would be too much for me. My fingers were never going to grip the whole thing.

As it continued to grow thicker, my fingers were forced to open up more space for its veiny surface to expand. It had now such a striking girth that my thumb lost its contact with my other fingers.

All the while, I continued to give him a handjob, not caring one bit that fear was still taking hold of me. I wanted to be calm in that situation, but it was simply impossible while my sight was more and more dominated by his growing package.

His shaft was now fully hard. It was so big that I had to blink twice. My poor mind could not grasp that such a thing existed.

"Suck it," he said, and I didn't need another invitation. My head moved down on the same instant, with my heart still pounding out of fear.

The moment I wrapped my lips around his bulbous cockhead, I knew that was what I had been born for. An Omega in heat like me just needed some good dick to worship before starting a day. My job had already started, but who's to say Hugo would not want me to come back, especially if he liked the blowjob?

Flip to the next page for more stories like this one.

MPREG SERIES AND MORE

SERIES - PREGNANT FOR HIM

1. Controlled by the Alpha 1: An MPREG Omegaverse Story
2. Controlled by the Alpha 2: An MPREG Omegaverse Story
3. Controlled by the Alpha 3: Dominating the Fertile Omega
4. Controlled by the Alpha 4: An Omega's Tale of Obedience
5. Controlled by the Alpha 5: A Tale of Obedient Submission
6. Controlled by the Alpha 6: Monopolized in Outer Space

SERIES - LOST INNOCENCE

1. Overwhelming the Omega 1: His Little Doll
2. Overwhelming the Omega 2: Brute Entry and Double Teamed
3. Overwhelming the Omega 3: His Tight Backdoor
4. Overwhelming the Omega 4: Stretching his Front Door
5. Overwhelming the Omega 5: Until he Spasms
6. Overwhelming the Omega 6: Naïve and Untouched

Straight to gay first time bundles:

1. Stuffed by Blue Collars: The Full Straight to Gay Age Gap Story

2. Throbbing Hard: A Straight to Gay MMF Bundle

3. Teasing Older Men: 16 Straight to Gay MM Stories

4. Helping Hand: 13 Forbidden Older Man Stories

5. So BIG It Hurts MEGA Bundle: 14 Stories of Man of the House, Brats and Gay Sitters

ABOUT THE AUTHOR

Michael Levi's biggest passion? Writing steamy, romantic stories that leave his readers panting. He's currently focusing on ABDL MM romances, but his collection is diverse and there are books for everyone's tastes. If you're looking for straight to gay, first time, BBC, sissification, and more, you're going to find them on his author page.

He lives to pamper his readers, every kiss means a lot more than what meets the eye, and he loves his Alpha males. Making sure that every gay first time feels different, Michael Levi writes his stories with a cup of coffee by his side. And for inspiration, he always opens up a photo of his new crush.